CHAPTER ONE

The Secret Seven had been
out together for a picnic.
Scamper was with them,
his tail wagging happily. He
loved being alone with Peter
and Janet – but it was even
better to be with the whole of

the Seven! There was always somebody fussing over him then, patting him, or talking to him.

'Well, I must say the hampers weigh a lot lighter coming *home* from a picnic than *going* to one!' said Janet, swinging hers to and fro. 'Oooh, sorry, Colin – didn't know you were just behind me.'

'You'd better give that to Scamper to carry,' said Colin. 'That's three times you've banged me with it.'

'Shall we go home through the fields or through the town?' said Peter.

'Through the town!' said everyone.

They were all thinking the same thing – what about a call at the ice-cream shop? So they went back through the town.

It was market-day and the streets were full. People rushed about here and there, carrying parcels, calling to one another, and cars had to go very slowly indeed because there were so

Enid Blyton

THE SECRET SEVEN

Hurry, Secret Seven, Hurry!

Illustrated by Tony Ross

working in
partnership
with

Hodder
Children's
Books

A division of Hachette Children's Books

Text copyright © Hodder & Stoughton Ltd 1956
Illustrations copyright © Hodder & Stoughton Ltd 2014

Made for McDonald's 2013. The following trademarks are owned by
McDonald's Corporation and its affiliates: McDonald's,
Happy Readers and The Golden Arches Logo.

The rights of Enid Blyton and Tony Ross to be identified as the Author and
Illustrator of the Work respectively have been asserted by them in accordance
with the Copyright, Designs and Patents Act 1988

The National Literacy Trust is a registered charity no: 1116260 and a company
limited by guarantee no. 5836826 registered in England and Wales and a
registered charity in Scotland no. SC042944. Registered address: 68 South
Lambeth Road, London SW8 1RL. National Literacy Trust logo and
reading tips © National Literacy Trust 2014
www.literacytrust.org.uk/donate

1

A Catalogue record for this book is available from the British Library

ISBN 978-1-444-91907-3

Typeset by Avon DataSet Ltd, Bidford on Avon, Warwickshire
Printed and bound in Germany by GGP Media GmbH, Pößneck (4)

The paper and board used in this paperback by Hodder Children's Books are
natural recyclable products made from wood grown in sustainable forests.
The manufacturing processes conform to the environmental regulations
of the country of origin.

Hodder Children's Books
a division of Hachette Children's Books
338 Euston Road, London NW1 3BH
An Hachette UK company
www.hachette.co.uk

many people walking in the road.

A man came down the street, cycling quickly. He rang his bell as if he were in a great

hurry, and people tried to get out of the way. Peter skipped to one side just in time as the man cycled past. He turned to stare after him indignantly.

'He almost knocked me over,' began Peter, and then stopped. Even as he spoke, something had happened.

CHAPTER TWO

CRASH! The man on the bicycle had bumped into a car and had been flung off into the road. A woman gave a loud scream and people hurried up at once.

The children ran to see what

had happened. The man lay there, half-dazed, his head badly bruised, and his cheek cut.

A policeman came up.

'He was going so *fast*,' said a woman nearby. 'He kept shouting to people to get out of the way. He was in an awful hurry and didn't seem to see that car.'

The man tried to speak and the policeman bent down. He listened hard and looked puzzled. 'He keeps saying

"Lever"', he said. 'Is that his name? Does anyone know?'

More people crowded up and the policeman began to send them off. 'Now, now — move away,' he said. 'Ah, here's a doctor. *Will* you move away, you kids? Give the poor fellow some room.'

The Secret Seven moved off with all the other children who had crowded round.

'I'll never ride *my* bicycle fast,' said Barbara. 'I never will, now I've seen how suddenly

accidents can happen.'

'Who was the man? Do you know?' asked Peter.

'I've never seen him before,' said Pam.

'Well, I seem to know his face,' said George, puzzled. 'Yes, I know I do. But I just can't think *who* he is.'

'*I* think I've seen him before, too,' said Jack, frowning. 'I've watched him doing something. What on earth can it be?'

'Oh, never mind,' said Pam. 'What does it matter? He's

in safe hands now, with a policeman there and a doctor.'

'I just *can't* remember,' said George. 'It's no good. I sort of feel he's something to do with the railway. He's not one of the porters, is he?'

'No,' said Jack, who knew all the porters because he so often went to meet his father off the train. 'He's not a porter – he's not the ticket-seller either, or the station-master. All the same, I can't help thinking you're right – he *is* something

to do with the railway.'

'Oh, stop bothering about it,' said Pam. 'I want to forget the accident. It was horrid.'

CHAPTER THREE

They walked along, swinging
their hampers and bags,
Peter and Colin arguing
about football, and the others
listening.

Suddenly George interrupted.

'I know! I've remembered who that man is!' he said. 'And we're right – he *is* something to do with the railway.'

'Is his name Lever?' asked Janet.

'No,' said George. '"Lever" is part of his work, though. He's the man who pulls the lever in the signal box when the train comes towards the railway station! You know – we've often watched him at the signal box, pulling the

lever to swing the big gates open and then shutting them over the line when the train has passed.'

'Oh *yes* – of course! You're right,' said Jack. 'It's Mr Williams!'

'I say – I hope there's someone who will pull the lever to open the gates for the next train!' said Peter, stopping suddenly. 'That's why he was in such a hurry, I expect. He wanted to get back in time to open the gates.'

'The six-fifteen is due soon,' said Colin. 'My father's on it!'

'Let's go back quickly and tell the policeman!' said Janet, suddenly feeling worried at the thought of a train racing along the lines and crashing into closed crossing-gates.

'No time,' said Colin, looking at his watch.

Peter made up his mind quickly. 'This may be serious,' he said. 'If there's no one at the station house to pull

the lever for the next train,
there'll certainly be a smash.
Even if the train doesn't rock
off the lines, those big gates
will be smashed to pieces.

Hurry up – we'll run to the signal box and find out if anyone is there.'

CHAPTER FOUR

The seven children, with
Scamper racing behind
barking excitedly, ran down
the road and round the corner.
Down the next road and up
a little hill and down again –
and there, some way in front

of them, stretched the railway-line.

'Keep going!' panted Peter. 'We're nearly there. We've still got a few minutes before the train is due.'

Peter reached the signal box first. It stood opposite the level-crossing, a pretty little place with a tiny garden of its own.

Peter yelled as he ran up to it. 'Is anyone there?'

He banged at the door and then rang the bell beside it.

Nobody answered.

Nobody came.

Then Colin ran to the window and looked inside. 'ANYONE IN?' he shouted at the top of his voice. He turned round. 'The signal box is empty!' he said. 'That's why Mr Williams was biking so fast to get back. He hadn't left anyone to see to the gates!'

'And that's why he kept saying "Lever! Lever!"' said Janet. 'What *are* we to do?'

'Pull the lever and open the

gates ourselves, of course,' said Peter, trying to be as calm as possible. He could see that the others were getting excited and alarmed. That would never do. Everyone must keep calm, everyone must help. They needed to get into the signal box as quickly as possible!

Colin looked round to see if anyone was near who could help them. A strong adult would be most welcome! But not a soul was there except a small girl, who stared at them solemnly all the time.

'George, Janet! Come with me to the door and help me to open it!' shouted Peter. 'Jack, you see if you can find another way in with Pam and Barbara and Colin. And for goodness sake, hurry up! The train's due in about a minute!'

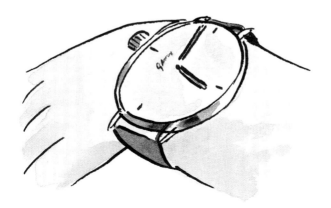

'We must all look out for it!' shouted Colin. 'It will be coming down the track at top speed before we know where we are!'

CHAPTER FIVE

Soon all seven children were
working hard to find a way
into the signal box. Peter
pushed at the door whilst
the others searched the
windowsills and the flower
beds for a spare key. It couldn't

only be Mr Williams who had a key!

'I can hear the train!' yelled Janet, who had very sharp ears. 'And the lines are beginning to tremble. Hurry, hurry!'

Colin was searching by the door when he found an upturned flowerpot. Inside, taped to the bottom, was a key.

'I've found it!' Colin called out with excitement.

'The train's coming!' shouted

Pam. 'The train's coming! Get inside, Peter, get inside!'

Yes – the train was certainly coming. It whistled as it came roaring along, and when Peter looked up he could see it coming down the line.

By this time Colin had got the signal box door open. Peter raced inside and found the lever. He grabbed it and pulled with all his might. Yes, the gates were opening! The train would be fine! Pam shouted again as the engine raced

past, making quite a wind.
Then the long row of swaying
carriages came rumbling past,
making a truly enormous
noise.

CHAPTER SIX

In a few moments the train had drawn into the station. People began to get off, all looking forward to getting home after a long day at work. Colin's father would be folding up his evening paper, ready to get off.

'I feel rather faint,' said
Barbara suddenly, and sat
down next to the lever. 'Oh
dear – how silly.'

'It's just the excitement,'

said Peter, whose heart was thumping so hard in his chest that he found it quite difficult to speak. 'My word, we didn't have much time. But we just did it!'

A shout came to their ears, and they turned. It was the policeman on a bicycle, with two or three men behind in a car.

'Hey – what are you doing, children? Did anything happen to the gates?'

'No. We managed to open

them for the train,' shouted
back Peter.

'Well, I'm amazed,' said
the policeman, getting off
his bicycle as the three men
jumped out of their car.

'Did you remember the lever
when you found out who that
man was who was knocked
down?' asked Peter.

'Yes – the fellow managed
to tell us at last,' said the
policeman. 'I shot off at once
– and these men came in their
car as soon as they could.

My word – when I saw the train racing by, I thought everything was up! I listened for the gates to be smashed – but no, the train just raced by as usual.'

'You mean to say you kids thought of the lever?' said one of the other men. 'How did you think of such a thing?'

'We remembered who that man was – Mr Williams, the crossing-gates man,' said George. 'Then we thought of the gates – and the train that was due – and we ran like hares to get to the signal box.'

'We only *just* managed it,' said Jack. 'Whew – I'm dripping wet! It was a long run!'

'I'm melting, too!' said Barbara, who was still sitting down, but already looking a little better.

CHAPTER SEVEN

'Who *are* you children?' said another man, a big, burly fellow, looking at them hard. 'You shouldn't be playing in the signal box.'

'We're the Secret Seven,' said Peter proudly, and tapped his

badge. 'Ready to do any job, at any time! But we wouldn't do anything too dangerous.'

'I'm a railway official,' said the man, 'and that was really a job for grown-ups, but you can take it from me that you've saved us pounds and pounds of damage by opening those gates – besides possibly a nasty accident. The train *might* have swerved off the rails if it had hit the gates.'

'I'm jolly glad it didn't,' said Colin. 'My father's on that train! Wait till I tell him our tale tonight!'

'Well, before you do that, I'd like you to do something else for me, if you will,' said the big man, and winked at the two other men who had been in the car with him.

'What's that?' asked Peter, with visions of another exciting bit of work to do. 'Help me to eat a few ice-creams!' said the man. 'You look so hot and bothered – you ought to cool down. And that

would be a good way of doing it – don't you think so?'

'Oooh yes!' said everyone.

Chapter Eight

The two men went to swing the gates back across the lines again, so that people might pass over on foot or in cars. The big man got into his car, and invited the children to follow him to the ice-cream shop just down the road.

Soon they were all sitting together, with such enormous ice-creams that they really couldn't believe their eyes.

'This is the biggest ice-cream I've ever had in my life,' said Peter.

'You deserve it, old son,' said the big man, who was eating an ice-cream, too.

'How in the world did you open those gates in time! You had only a few minutes to race away from Mr Williams, get

into the signal box, and pull the lever. I don't know *how* you did it!'

'Yes – you're right,' said Peter, thinking about it. '*I* don't quite know how we did it, either. But the thing is – we *did* it!'

Well, that's really all that matters, Secret Seven. You saw what had to be done – and YOU DID IT!

FUN AND GAMES WITH THE SECRET SEVEN

Turn over for exciting
Secret Seven activities
(you'll find the
answers on page 64).

CO-ORDINATE CONFUSION

The station master's bumped his head and forgotten his name. Help the Secret Seven work it out by matching the co-ordinates to the letters below.

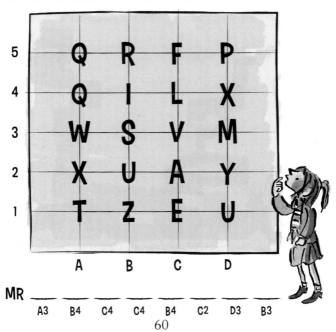

MR ___ ___ ___ ___ ___ ___ ___
   A3 B4 C4 C4 B4 C2 D3 B3

TRAINSPOTTING

Jack's dad is arriving on the busiest train. Can you help Jack work out which train his dad is on by spotting the train with the most passengers?

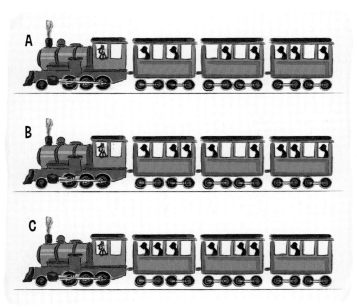

ROUTE TO
THE RAILWAY

The Secret Seven need to get to the signal box as quickly as possible to open the gate! Who's taken the right route?

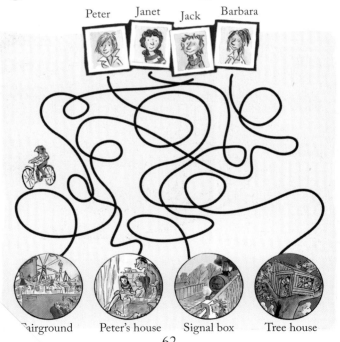

Peter   Janet   Jack   Barbara

Fairground   Peter's house   Signal box   Tree house

SCAMPER'S DOT-TO-DOT

Complete the dot-to-dot to find out what Scamper's carrying in his mouth. Then colour the picture in.

ANSWERS PAGE

CO-ORDINATE CONFUSION

MR <u>W</u> <u>I</u> <u>L</u> <u>L</u> <u>I</u> <u>A</u> <u>M</u> <u>S</u>
   A3 B4 C4 C4 B4 C2 D3 B3

TRAINSPOTTING

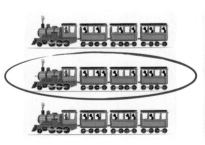

ROUTE TO THE RAILWAY

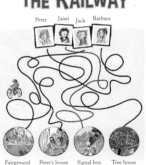

Peter   Janet   Jack   Barbara

Fairground   Peter's house   Signal box   Tree house